PLEASE, MALESE!

A TRICKSTER TALE FROM HAITI

BY AMY MacDONALD / PICTURES BY EMILY LISKER

MELANIE KROUPA BOOKS

FARRAR STRAUS GIROUX / NEW YORK

Distributed in Canada by Douglas & McIntyre Ltd.
Color separations by Hong Kong Scanner Arts
Printed and bound in the United States of America by Berryville Graphics
Designed by Sylvia Frezzolini Severance
First edition, 2002
1 3 5 7 9 10 8 6 4 2

Library of Congress Cataloging-in-Publication Data
MacDonald, Amy.
    Please, Malese! : a trickster tale from Haiti / by Amy MacDonald ; pictures by
Emily Lisker.— 1st ed.
        p.   cm.
    Summary: Using his tricky ways, Malese takes advantage of his neighbors, until
they catch on, after which he manages to pull an even bigger trick on them.
    ISBN 0-374-36000-6
    [1. Folklore—Haiti. 2. Tricksters—Folklore.] I. Lisker, Emily, ill. II. Title.

PZ8.1.M1592 Pl 2002
398.2'097294'02—dc21
[E]
                                                                              2001029386

For K.C.
—A.M.

For Samantha with love,
and special thanks to Melanie, Sylvia, and Bill
—E.L.

Malese was lying in his hammock one day when he noticed that his shoes were all worn out.

"My toes are suffering," said Malese. "They need new shoes, that's what they need." He looked around his humble cottage. He had no money and nothing to trade. But Malese did not despair. Instead he went to town and found a shoemaker.

"Makak," he said, "I need new shoes. But I'm mighty particular about my shoes. They must be just so. You make me a left shoe, and bring it to my house. If it's good, why then you can make me the other one, too."

So Makak made him a shoe—exactly as Malese had described it—and brought it to his house.

"That's a terrible shoe!" Malese cried. "It's ugly as a horned toad. Take it back."

"Take it back?" said Makak. "Now, who else gonna wear a shoe like that?" And he flung it into the bamboo bushes and went away.

Now Malese went back to town and found another shoemaker. He asked Cabrit to do the same thing, but this time he asked for a right shoe. So Cabrit made him a shoe. But when he saw it, Malese shook his head sadly.

"That's a horrible shoe," he said. "It's ugly as a blister. You can take it back."

"Now, who else gonna want that shoe?" cried Cabrit. And he flung it into the bamboo bushes and went away.

Just so did Malese get a brand-new pair of shoes, and himself not a penny poorer for it.

Next day was market day, and Malese was hungry.

"My stomach is suffering," he declared. "It needs rum cake, that's what it needs." And his mouth watered as he thought of his favorite cake: sweet, fragrant, and covered in white icing.

But Malese had no rum for a cake, and no money to buy rum. Still, he did not despair. Instead he took an empty bottle and filled it half up with water.

Then he walked through the marketplace until he saw his neighbor Bouki.

"Bouki," he said, "my rum's half gone. Fill my bottle up, brother."

Bouki looked at Malese. Malese had tricked him many, many times before. But he could see no trick in this. So he got his big jug of clear white rum and filled Malese's bottle with it. Then he counted on his fingers.

"That'll be two dollars," he said, holding out his hand.

"Two dollars?" cried Malese with astonishment. He held the bottle behind his back and swirled it until the rum and water were all mixed up. "Why, that's daylight robbery! I got no two dollars! Here, you take your miserable rum back!"

And he poured half his bottle back into Bouki's jug. Then he walked along the marketplace till he saw another rum merchant.

"Zwazo," he said, "fill my bottle up, sister." Zwazo looked at
Malese. She didn't trust him, either. But she got her jug and filled
Malese's bottle.
"That'll be two dollars," said Zwazo.

"Two dollars? Two dollars!" cried Malese, dancing in anger
and shaking the bottle over his head. "Why, that's daylight robbery!
I've a mind to call the police. Here, you take your miserable rum back!"

And he poured half his bottle back into Zwazo's jug.
Then he continued along the market. And every place he stopped,
he filled his bottle with rum, jumped and shouted and swirled
and twirled the bottle—and poured half of it back again. By the
time he got to the end of the market, his bottle, which had
once been half full of water, was now half full of rum.
And Malese was not a penny poorer.

The walk home was long and steep. Soon Malese began to tire. "My legs are suffering," said Malese. "They need a rest, that's what they need." Just then he saw Bouki coming, leading a donkey piled high with baskets from the market. Malese saw his chance.

"Bouki," he called, "have you no mercy? Your poor donkey is suffering under that load. Why, it's bigger than he is." This was only half true, for though the load of baskets was big, it was light. But Bouki was not clever and he did not think about this.

"What you want me to do, carry it for him?" snapped Bouki.

"Never, brother, never!" said Malese, flinging up his hands. "I just feel sorry for the poor little bourik."

"Ha!" cried Bouki. "You so tender, why don't *you* carry his load for him, then?"

Malese frowned. He struck his forehead with his fist. "Bouki!" he moaned. "You too smart for me. You trick me with my own words. All right, you win."

So saying, he climbed onto the donkey
and balanced the load of baskets on his own head.
Off they went up the steep mountainside, Bouki
toiling in the hot sun, Malese riding in splendor.
And all the time Bouki smiled to himself, thinking
that for once he had outwitted Malese.

Malese arrived home cool and rested
and quickly made his rum cake—
sweet and fragrant and
covered in white icing.

But that afternoon the villagers got to talking among themselves.
Cabrit told Makak about the shoes. Zwazo told Bouki about the rum.
And so it happened that just as Malese sat down to eat his cake,
he saw a big crowd a-coming. They looked madder than boiled owls.